The Little Lost Sheep

written by Marilyn Lee Lindsey
illustrated by Ruth A. O'Connell

2nd paperback printing, 1998
Library of Congress Catalog Card No. 87-91993
© 1988, The Standard Publishing Company, Cincinnati, Ohio. All rights reserved.
A division of Standex International Corporation. Printed in the U.S.A.

Once there was a baby sheep who lived with his warm, woolly mother. They lived on a hill with lots of other warm, woolly sheep.

One spring morning the baby sheep decided to take a walk. He wanted to take a walk to see the world that God had made.

The baby sheep walked down the other side of the hill. He looked on the ground. He saw a tiny crocus poking through the soft dirt.

And he was glad.

The baby sheep looked between two rocks. He saw a big, green woolly worm peeking out of the crack.

And he was glad.

The baby sheep walked around a prickly bush that had lots of big thorns on it. He walked on down a rocky hillside. He stopped. He looked back up the hill. Where was his grassy, hill home? Where was his warm, woolly mother?

Then the baby sheep saw a sparrow sitting on a twig of the prickly bush. He asked the tiny bird, "Can you help me find my way home? I want my grassy, hill home. I need my warm, woolly mother."

The sparrow said to the baby sheep,
"Don't worry, the good shepherd will
find you and take you safely home."

Walking on, the baby sheep saw a lily growing among the grass. He asked the tall, slender flower, "Can you help me find my way home? I want my grassy, hill home. I need my warm, woolly mother."

The lily said to the baby sheep,
"Don't worry, the good shepherd will
find you and take you safely home."

As he walked on, the baby sheep saw a badger climbing over some rocks. He asked the small, furry animal, "Can you help me find my way home? I want my grassy, hill home. I need my warm, woolly mother."

The badger said to the baby sheep,
"Don't worry, the good shepherd will
find you and take you safely home."

But the baby sheep was now so tired, he lay down against a rock and began to cry. He was all alone and afraid. Who could take him safely home?

Then the baby sheep heard something. He stopped crying and lifted his head. Someone was calling to him.

"Come to me, Little One," said the good shepherd. "I will take you safely home again."

The baby sheep ran to the shepherd. And the good shepherd gently lifted the baby sheep into his strong arms. He carried the baby sheep to his grassy, hill home. He was safely home again with his warm, woolly mother.

And he was glad.

Fingerplay Fun: Five Little Sheep

(Hold up index finger)  This little sheep said,
  "I just love to eat."

(Add middle finger) This little sheep said,
  "This grass tastes so sweet."

(Add ring finger) This little sheep said,
  "A drink of water for me."

(Add little finger) This little sheep said,
  "I'll nap under this tree."

(Wiggle thumb) But this little sheep said,
  "I'm so lonely out in the
  dark and the cold."

*(Use other hand to
fold thumb into palm
of hand; then fold the
fingers over thumb)* Then the good shepherd brought
  him back safely to his friends
  in the fold.